A Friend Is Someone Who Likes You

JOAN WALSH ANGLUND

A

Friend

Is

Someone

Who

Likes

You

Harcourt, Inc.

Orlando   Austin   New York   San Diego   London

By Joan Walsh Anglund

Requests for permission to make copies of any part of the work should
be submitted online at www.harcourt.com/contact or mailed
to the following address: Permissions Department,
Houghton Mifflin Harcourt Publishing Company,
6277 Sea Harbor Drive, Orlando, Florida 32887-6777.

www.HarcourtBooks.com

Library of Congress Cataloging-in-Publication Data
Anglund, Joan Walsh.
A friend is someone who likes you/Joan Walsh Anglund.
p.   cm.
Summary: Text and illustrations describe what a friend is.
[1. Friendship—Fiction.]   I. Title.
PZ7.A586Fr   1993
[E]—dc20   92-22609
ISBN 978-0-15-229678-0

O Q S U V T R P

Manufactured in China

for Bob, Joy, and Todd because they helped

A friend is someone who likes you.

It can be a boy . . .

It can be a girl . . .

or a cat . . .

or a dog . . .

or even a white mouse.

A tree can be a different kind of friend.
It doesn't talk to you, but you know it
likes you, because it gives you apples . . .
or pears . . . or cherries . . .
or, sometimes, a place to swing.

A brook can be a friend in a special way.
It talks to you with splashy gurgles.
It cools your toes and lets you sit
quietly beside it when you don't feel
like speaking.

The wind can be a friend too.
It sings soft songs to you at night
    when you are sleepy and feeling lonely.
Sometimes it calls to you to play.
It pushes you from behind
as you walk and makes
the leaves dance for you.
It is always with you
    wherever you go,
    and that's how you know
    it likes you.

Sometimes you don't know who
        are your friends.
Sometimes they are there all the time,
but you walk right past them
and don't notice that they like you
        in a special way.

And then you think you don't have any
friends.

Then you must stop hurrying and rushing
so fast . . .

and move very slowly,
and look around carefully,
to see someone who smiles at you
in a special way . . .
or a dog that wags its tail extra hard
whenever you are near . . .
or a tree that lets you climb it easily . . .
or a brook that lets you be quiet
when you want to be quiet.
Sometimes you have to find your friend.

Some people have lots and lots of friends . .

and some people have quite a few friends . . .

but everyone . . .
everyone in the whole world
has at least *one* friend.

Where did you find yours?